CITIES OF SOUTH AMERICA

LIZ GOGERLY AND ROB HUNT

ILLUSTRATED BY
VICTOR BEUREN

W
FRANKLIN WATTS
LONDON · SYDNEY

Franklin Watts
First published in Great Britain in 2021
by The Watts Publishing Group

Copyright © The Watts Publishing Group 2021

Credits
Artwork by Victor Beuren
Design: Collaborate Agency
Editor: Nicola Edwards

ISBN 978 1 4451 6895 1 (hb); 978 1 4451 6896 8 (pb)

Printed in Dubai

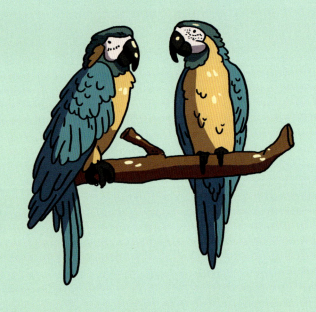

Franklin Watts
An imprint of
Hachette Children's Group
Part of the Watts Publishing Group
Carmelite House
50 Victoria Embankment
London EC4Y 0DZ

An Hachette UK Company
www.hachette.co.uk

www.franklinwatts.co.uk

CONTENTS

CITIES OF SOUTH AMERICA

South America is the fourth-largest continent with a total area of roughly 17,814,000 square kilometres, which is about one eighth of the land on Earth. The estimated population of the continent is 438.7 million, making it the third most populated of all the continents.

South America gets its name from Amerigo Vespucci (1454–1512), the intrepid Italian explorer who made voyages to the continent in 1499 and 1501. It was Vespucci who realised that the coastline he was exploring wasn't Asia but another 'new' continent. Of course it wasn't new – the land was inhabited by indigenous people, including the mighty Incas. However, to the Europeans it was the 'New World'...

Cuzco, the historic capital of the Inca Empire

The Portuguese and Spanish lost little time in colonising most of this exciting 'new' continent with its promise of gold and other riches (the British and Dutch tried too in Suriname and Guyana). Most South American countries took back independence in the nineteenth century, but many of the cities have echoes of their colonial past. Portuguese is the most widely spoken language with Spanish a near second. The buildings, food, culture and way of life are heavily influenced by those European settlers.

CARACAS

CARTAGENA

GEORGETOWN

PARAMARIBO

BOGOTÁ

QUITO

CUENCA

MANAUS

LIMA

CUZCO

LA PAZ

SANTA CRUZ

POTOSÍ

RIO DE JANEIRO

ASUNCIÓN

SANTIAGO

MONTEVIDEO

BUENOS AIRES

Cuenca in Ecuador is famous for its beautiful colonial buildings and its city centre is a UNESCO World Heritage Site.

Brazil is the most populated country in South America and São Paulo is its most populated city. This super-busy, multi-cultural city has over 21.7 million people, making it the 12th most populated city in the world. It isn't a pretty city but like many South American cities it is exciting and full of life. The official language is Portuguese so don't forget to say 'Olá!'.

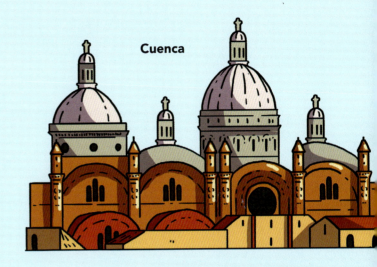

Cuenca

Tango dancers

Buenos Aires in Argentina is often ranked the most popular city with tourists to South America. An estimated 2 million visitors come to this beautiful city to soak up its art and architecture. It also claims to be the birthplace of tango dancing and is known for its sizzling steaks. Spanish is the most widely spoken language so greet people with 'Hola!'.

The Andes Mountains sweep along the western edge of South America and you get some of the highest cities in the world on its ridges. La Paz in Bolivia at 3,640 m is the highest capital city on Earth. La Rinconada in Peru at 5,130 m is the highest settlement (sometimes referred to as city) in the world. It's cold and barren but there is gold in the mountains so people keep moving here!

There are so many exciting cities with rich historical pasts for you to explore in South America. Whether you're into dancing, food, football, awesome mountain views, golden beaches or discovering beautiful old buildings you're in for a good time. So grab your bags and your passport and let's go!

La Paz

Rio has some of the most famous **beaches** in the world. The long, white sands of **Ipanema** and **Copacabana** are often packed with surfers, sunbathers and people playing football or volleyball.

The **Sugarloaf Mountain** peak (so-called because it looks like an old-fashioned cone of sugar) is situated on a peninsula at the mouth of Guanabara Bay. The mountain peaks at 396 m and you can reach the top via two cable cars. The cable cars appear in many films, including the James Bond classic *Moonraker*.

Mount Corcovado is a 710-m-tall rocky peak surrounded by Tijuca Forest National Park. Corcovado actually means 'hunchback', which refers to the distinct shape of the mountain. Take the red narrow-gauge train to the top and you can see over the city out to the ocean.

Rio lies on the western shores of **Guanabara Bay.** The bay itself is 31 km long and measures 28 km wide at its broadest. There are over 130 islands in the bay and the port of Rio de Janeiro and its two main airports are situated on its shoreline.

On top of Mount Corcovado is the world-renowned statue **Christ the Redeemer**. The 30-m statue was made in France by the Polish sculptor Paul Landowski and inaugurated in 1931. Jesus has his arms wide open as if he's blessing the entire city.

President Costa e Silva Bridge crosses the bay and connects Rio with the city of Niterói. It's 13.29 km long, making it the sixth-longest concrete bridge of its kind in the world.

Barra da Tijuca Beach is the longest beach in the city stretching for 18 km. It has some mega waves so lots of international surfing competitions take place here.

RIO DE JANEIRO

BRAZIL

Oi, tudo bem? ('Hi, how are you?' in Portuguese) from Rio de Janeiro, the second-most populated city in Brazil, and one of the friendliest places on Earth. There are around 6.7 million people living in the centre with an estimated 13.5 million in the greater metropolitan area. Residents of the city are known as *cariocas* and they have a great love of the beach, samba dancing and football.

The **Barra Olympic Park** was built for the Summer Olympics hosted by Rio in 2016. Unfortunately, the nine buildings that were specially commissioned for the Games have since been abandoned.

Maracana Stadium was the biggest stadium in the world when it was opened in 1950. The 78,000-seat stadium has been used for football tournaments including the World Cup in 1950 and 2014. The iconic stadium was last used for the 2016 Summer Olympics.

Rio is famous for its slum neighbourhoods, called favelas. The city has around more than 600 favelas and the largest is **Rocinha** to the south. Around 180,000 people are crammed into makeshift, box-like houses in this slum alone.

In the centre of Rio stands the **Carioca Aqueduct**. It was built in the eighteenth century by Portuguese colonists to carry water from the Carioca river to the city and it has been used as a bridge for trams since the nineteenth century.

Rio de Janeiro Cathedral is one of the most unusual cathedrals you will ever see. The concrete structure was inspired by ancient Aztec design but looks totally modern. It was built between 1964 and 1979 and has magnificent stained glass windows.

HISTORY

Rio de Janeiro (translates as 'river of January') was named by the Portuguese explorer Gaspar de Lemos, who landed here in January 1502. The Portuguese encountered indigenous peoples (the Guarani and Tupinambá) who had lived in this area long before the arrival of the Europeans. Nevertheless the Portuguese decided to found a city of their own here. Over the centuries Rio de Janeiro has prospered on sugarcane, brazilwood, gold and later coffee. The Portuguese ruled but the city's fortune was built through the hard work of slaves brought from Africa. Today, Rio is a vibrant city which reflects the European influence and its multi-cultural past.

MONEY

The Brazilian real is the official currency of Brazil. It was introduced to Brazil in 1994 and is the strongest currency in South America. Special commemorative 1 real coins were made to celebrate the 2016 Olympic Games in Rio.

Apothecary's Square

 ## PLACES TO GO

Largo do Boticário

Get a taste of old Rio at **Largo do Boticário (Apothecary's Square)**. This charming square was built in the eighteenth century by Portuguese colonists. The buildings are painted in vibrant colours and covered in tropical plants. Many of them are abandoned but people hope the area will be rejuvenated.

Tijuca National Park

Once Rio was surrounded by rainforest and at the **Tijuca National Park** you can get an idea of how beautiful it must have been. There are waterfalls, caves, craggy rocks, towering trees and tropical plants. There are also cheeky capuchin monkeys and pretty little birds, like the eye-ringed tody-tyrant or red-necked tanager, to spot.

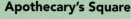

Animals at the Tijuca Forest National Park

FOOD

Chocolate!

If you love chocolate then **brigadeiros** are for you! These balls are made from cacao powder, condensed milk, butter and eggs and coated in chocolate sprinkles. Pistachio nuts, almonds, coconut and strawberries are sometimes added too.

Brigadeiros

THINGS TO DO

Take part in carnival celebrations

The **Rio Carnival** is the biggest festival in the world and is celebrated every year before Lent (February or March). Major parades take place at an open-air venue called the Sambódromo. It gets packed with colourful floats and people in bright, glittery costumes. The sound of steel bass drums and samba rhythms fill the air. It's a full-on celebration that spreads to the streets of the city and ends in parties and carnival balls everywhere.

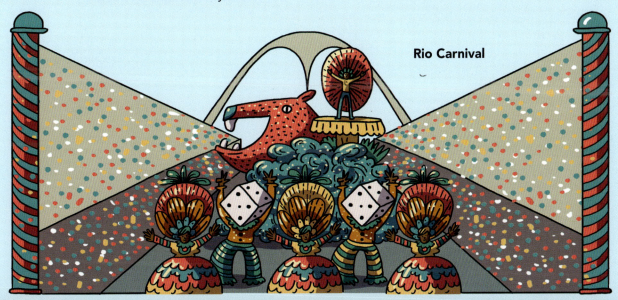

Rio Carnival

Bogotá is near the Equator but because it is so high up the weather is milder than you'd expect - Colombians call the city 'the Fridge'. Expect fog, grey skies and don't be surprised if you feel out of breath because of the altitude.

The **white chapel** at the top of **Monserrate** was built by the Spanish in 1640 and is still a popular place for people on religious pilgrimages.

The city is quite easy to get around because it is mostly laid out in a grid pattern. The streets have numbers rather than names. *Carreras* are avenues that run north to south. *Calles* are the streets that run east to west.

The **National Capitol** building is used by Colombian congress. The neoclassical building took 80 years to complete and was finally finished in 1926.

La Candelaria is the historic centre of the city. Many of the older buildings are in the Spanish colonial style but there are modern galleries, art centres and libraries to explore too. Hidden within the cobbled alleyways are interesting shops, restaurants and street art.

Plaza de Bolívar is the main square in La Candelaria. The tourists and pigeons flock here! The square dates back to 1539 and has been used for markets, bullfights and circus performances.

BOGOTÁ
COLOMBIA

Buenas from Bogotá, the capital and the most populous city in Colombia with around 11 million people. Emerald mountains (the tallest is Monserrate Hill) surround Bogotá, which is located on a plateau around 2,640 metres above sea level on the Eastern Ranges of the Andes. Tourists who come to Bogotá enjoy exploring its historic centre and experience its contemporary art and music scene.

Opposite the National Capitol building stands the **Primatial Cathedral of Bogotá**. There have been four cathedrals on this site including the original thatched chapel from 1565. The neoclassical cathedral you see today was completed in 1823.

Chapinero is the financial and commercial heart of Bogotá. The Colombia Stock Exchange Building is slick and modern. There are shiny new shopping centres and plenty of up-market restaurants, too.

HISTORY

In 1538 the Spanish conquistadors invaded and laid claim to the land that belonged to the indigenous Muisca Bogotá. By 1717 Bogotá was the capital of the Spanish colony New Granada and it remained the capital when Colombia took back independence in 1819. Civil wars, strikes and struggles are just part of Bogotá's interesting history. So are culture, art and learning which have earned this city the nickname 'Athens of South America'.

MONEY

The local currency is the Colombian peso (COL$). The notes come in denominations of $1,000 up to $100,000. A cup of coffee costs around $3,000, which is the equivalent of around $0.80 USD.

Mural by the artist known as Stinkfish

THINGS TO DO

See some art

Art is everywhere in this city. Graffiti is legal in some parts of Bogotá. There are special tours to show visitors the most interesting examples, such as this portrait of a stranger, by the artist Stinkfish brought to life by vibrant colourful patterns typical of his style.

Fernando Botero is one of Colombia's most famous artists and sculptors. He is best known for his large comical figures. You can see 123 of his works at the Museo Botero, including *The Hand*, a perfect example of 'Boterismo', the artist's signature style of depicting figures and events with exaggerated and disproportionate dimensions.

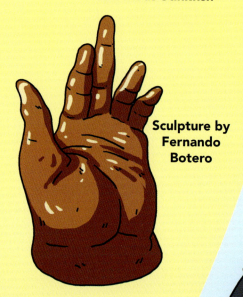

Sculpture by Fernando Botero

FOOD

Coffee ...

Colombia is the third-largest producer of coffee in the world and used to export most of the good quality beans. Now it keeps some and there are coffee shops all over Bogotá. The coffee is so good it is often drunk without milk, cream or sugar!

... and drinking chocolate

Chocolate is more likely to be drunk than eaten in Colombia. In Bogotá people have hot chocolate for breakfast at home or at a bakery with a savoury pastry called an *arepa*. They love to dunk cheese in their chocolate, too!

Coffee shop

Hot chocolate

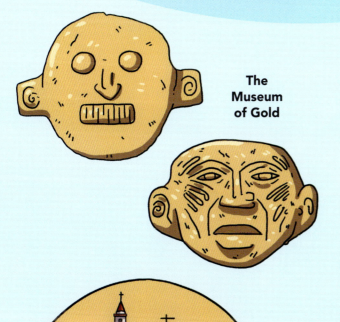

The Museum of Gold

PLACES TO GO

El Museo del Oro (The Museum of Gold)
Inside El Museo del Oro is a treasure trove of gold artifacts. The museum has 55,000 pieces, including masks, jewellery, figures and other works by the indigenous Muisca people.

The best view of the city is from the top of **Monserrate**. It takes over an hour to walk to the summit which, at 3,152 metres, is pretty high up! You can save your legs (and breath) and take the funicular or cable car instead.

Monserrate

Get up early to see the sunrise from the mountain. Since long before the Spanish arrived, the indigenous Muisca people have considered Monserrate to be a sacred place. The Sun rises from directly behind the mountain during the summer solstice in June.

Head to **San Cristóbal Hill** in the north of the city for an awesome view of the city and the mighty peaks of the Andes in the near distance. The hill is around 300 metres above the city, so you can take a cable car or climb aboard the funicular to reach the top.

San Cristobal is within Santiago's large green **Parque Metropolitano.** The park has a zoo, a botanical garden, water fountains and swimming pools. The white statue of the Virgin Mary stands at 14 metres tall and looks out over the city.

Plaza de Armas has been the main square in the city ever since it was founded by the Spanish in 1541. Its name translates as 'Weapons Square'. The Spanish planned many of their towns on a grid system, leaving a square in the centre. Important buildings were erected around the square. The idea was if the city were under attack then people could gather at the square to take arms against the enemy. Today the square is a great place to catch up on history or just sit in a street cafe and watch the world go by!

A series of powerful earthquakes (in 1647, 1657 and 1730) decimated parts of Santiago so many of the buildings that you see in the Plaza de Armas were built in the nineteenth century.

A cathedral has stood at the site of the **Santiago Metropolitan Cathedral** since the mid-fourteenth century. This ornate building was opened in 1800 with many parts added later.

The **Central Post Office Building** was built between 1881–1908 and is possibly one of the grandest post offices in the world. It has a museum with a large collection of stamps, too.

SANTIAGO
CHILE

The **Palacio de la Real Audiencia** was completed in 1808 and in the past has been used as a seat for government and home for the President. Now it houses the Chilean National History Museum.

Buenos dias from Santiago, the capital city of Chile. This busy city is in a valley but look up and there are mountains all around. Just over 5 million people live in the city with over 6 million in the metropolitan area – that is roughly 40 per cent of the population of Chile. Santiago was founded by the Spanish in the sixteenth century, so expect beautiful old buildings. However, this is a financial and economic hub with an eye to the future.

Gran Torre Santiago is the second-tallest building in Latin America. It is 300 metres tall and was completed in 2013. A super-fast lift whisks you to the observation deck called 'Sky Costanera' in just two minutes. At the top you get a fabulous view across Santiago and the Andes.

The muddy **Mapocho River** winds through the city, dividing it in two.

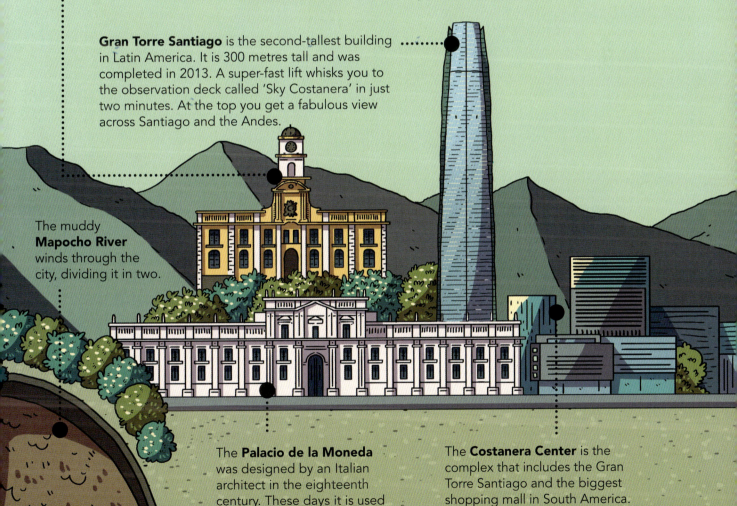

The **Palacio de la Moneda** was designed by an Italian architect in the eighteenth century. These days it is used by the president of Chile, but tourists are allowed to have a look at some of the grand rooms inside.

The **Costanera Center** is the complex that includes the Gran Torre Santiago and the biggest shopping mall in South America. The mall has six floors with hundreds of shops, a cinema, gym and food hall to seat 2,000 people.

HISTORY

Santiago is one of the most successful cities in South America. Fertile soil and a temperate climate makes it perfect for agriculture. However, it was the mountain setting (high ground is easier to defend) and position on the Mapocho River that made it attractive to the Spanish conquistadors back in the fourteenth century. Pedro de Valdivia founded the city in 1541 and the local Pecunche Indians were placed under Spanish rule. There are hints of Santiago's colonial past all over the city but Chile claimed back its country and its capital in 1810. The fight for independence, devastating earthquakes and a terrifying military coup in 1973 have shaken Santiago. However, it has survived and thrived to become one of the most popular places to visit in South America.

MONEY

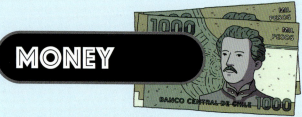

The Chilean peso is the official currency of Chile.

PLACES TO GO

La Vega Central Market

The largest indoor market in Chile is bursting with life as well as fruit, vegetables and flowers. This is a good place to eat traditionally cooked Chilean food.

Cementerio General de Santiago

This is one of the largest cemeteries in South America, with beautiful statues, chapels and fountains commemorating the dead. Many famous people are buried here, including President Salvador Allende.

Stall at La Vega Central Market

Graveyard memorials

FOOD

Smoothies

Chilli in Chile

Sopaipilla is sold all over the city. These orange-coloured pastries are fried in hot oil. You choose the sauce – the most famous is called pebre and it's packed with fiery chilli peppers!

Sopaipillas

Juicy fruits

In Santiago there are juice bars everywhere. Chile is the top exporter of fruit in South America and they have bumper crops of grapes, plums, pears, apples and peaches. Tropical fruits such as papaya, chirimoya and pepino are key exports too. This all makes for some delicious and distinctive blends of juice and smoothies.

THINGS TO DO

Visit the Open Air Museum of San Miguel

This amazing community project was created to revitalise the run-down neighbourhood of San Miguel. The beautiful murals of the Open Air Museum tell stories about the city and its history. La Mano's mural *Latinoamerica* depicts the rich cultural diversity of South America.

'Latinoamerica' mural by La Mano

The tallest buildings are the twin **Central Park Towers**. They are 225 m tall and form part of a large residential, commercial and cultural complex. The towers were opened in the early 1980s and are an iconic feature of the Caracas skyline.

The **National Pantheon of Venezuela** is the final resting place of many famous Venezuelans. Simón Bolívar, known as 'The Liberator' because he led the movement to free large parts of Latin America from the Spanish Empire in the early nineteenth century, is buried here.

Another stand-out building is **El Helicoide**, a rounded, pyramid-style building that was originally intended to be a shopping mall in the early 1960s. The mall was never completed and the government took it over and finished building it in the 1980s. It is now used by the government security services as a prison.

CARACAS
VENEZUELA

Hola, or *hello*, from Caracas, the largest city and capital of Venezuela. This is a city of contrasts; it lies in a valley on the Guaire River and is overlooked by the Venezuelan Andes mountain range but it is also not far from the Caribbean coastline. Around 3 million people live in this hectic city, including immigrants from Europe, the Middle East, China and other Latin American countries.

One of the striking features of the Caracas skyline is the **Tower of David**. Building started in 1990, but money ran out in 1994 and the 190-m-tall skyscraper was left unfinished. Squatters took up residence there from 2007–2015, peaking at 5,000 occupants, who had a system of shops, water to the 10th floor, and a taxi service!

There is a statue of **Simón Bolívar** at the centre of the **Plaza Bolívar**. It's surrounded by greenery and beautiful Spanish colonial architecture. The building highlights include the **Federal Legislative Palace**, **Caracas Cathedral**, and the **Palacio Municipal de Caracas**.

HISTORY

On 25 July 1567, Captain Diego de Losada declared, "I take possession of this land in the name of God and the King" and named the city Santiago de León de Caracas. In fact, Caracas was the name of the indigenous people who had been there for centuries before the Europeans arrived. Spain ruled the area until Simón Bolívar rebelled and won independence in 1811. It was a small and modest capital until 1914 when oil was discovered – the population boomed and it developed into a modern and thriving capital. However, the economy was too dependent on oil and when worldwide oil prices dropped, the Venezuelan economy crashed leading to high levels of poverty and crime in the city.

MONEY

Until 2018 the official currency was the bolívar fuerte, named after the independence leader Simón Bolívar. Fuerte means strong but the currency was not strong enough and lost its value very quickly – it eventually cost 3 million bolivars to buy a bunch of carrots! Since 2018, the currency in Venezuela has been the bolívar soberano, but many people are using dollars or euros because bolivars devalue so quickly.

THINGS TO DO

Experience culture in Caracas

Caracas is a centre of culture in the area and the biggest symbol of that is the **Teresa Carreño Cultural Complex.** It was opened in 1983 and named after a famous pianist. It is a great place to see plays, concerts, opera and ballet.

Relax in the Botanical Garden

You can escape the crowds at the **Botanical Garden of Caracas**. This large green space in the centre of the city is home to many different plant species from across the world. You may be lucky enough to see toucans, macaws and other parrots!

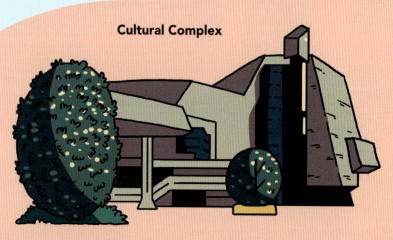

Cultural Complex

Parrots

FOOD

Beef, capybara or crocodile?

Venezuelan cuisine is diverse because of its immigrant population. One of the most popular dishes is heavily influenced by Caribbean cuisine. **Pabellón criollo** is a version of rice and beans with shredded beef. It is often served with slices of plantain and if you don't like beef you can substitute that with capybara or crocodile meat.

Levantón Andino

Pabellón criollo

Bull's eye cocktail

Those with a strong stomach might like to wash this all down with a refreshing drink of **levantón andino**. Its ingredients include bull's eyes, fish eggs, chicken eggs and quail eggs!

PLACES TO GO

Ávila National Park

The Teleférico is a cable car that takes visitors to a mountain top in the Ávila National Park. En route, you can see a variety of butterflies, birds and orchids. At the top is the Humboldt Hotel. The 60-m, circular tower was built in 1956 but was later abandoned. It reopened in 2018 and you can experience the wonderful views from the hotel's viewing stations.

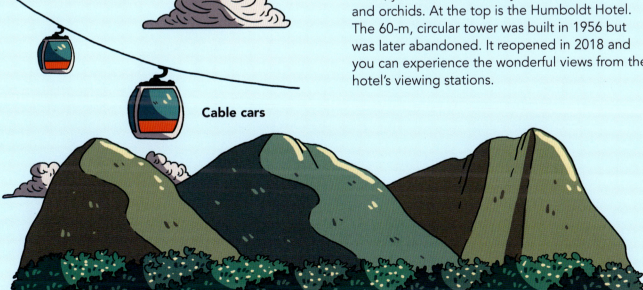

Cable cars

Quito is the only capital in the world that is built on a volcano. **Pichincha** is still active with three major eruptions in the past 2,000 years. Scientists suggest there is a 40 per cent chance it could erupt again soon. This must be worrying for the 2 million people that live in the city.

Quito is perched 2,850 metres above sea level. You can take a cable car up the side of Pichincha and go even higher! The **Teleférico** rises to 3,945 metres, making it one of the highest cable cars in the world. Some days it gets a bit cloudy up there and, because of the altitude, it gets quite chilly and you may feel dizzy.

A magnificent statue of the Virgin Mary (**La Virgen del Panecillo**) watches from high on El Panecillo hill – she looks like she's been here forever but she was only unveiled in 1975. She is the tallest statue of Mary with wings in the world (she's 38 m tall) and you can see her from most parts of the city.

Independence Square (**Plaza de la Independencia**) is at the heart of the old town. The monument in the middle commemorates independence from Spanish rule in 1822.

Quito was the first city to be declared a UNESCO World Heritage Site in 1978. The city's **old town** is packed with churches, colonial buildings and plazas. It's closed to traffic for much of the day so you can explore its cobbled streets by foot or bike.

QUITO
ECUADOR

The striking white **Cathedral of Quito** also graces the square. A church has been on this site since 1534 when the city was founded by the Spanish. Earthquakes and volcanoes have destroyed previous churches. The cathedral you see today dates from the seventeenth century.

Hola! and welcome to Quito, the second-highest capital (beaten only by La Paz in Bolivia) in the world. Quito is also the closest capital city to the Equator and the only one which straddles the Southern and Northern Hemispheres. Its unique position means there are just two seasons in this city: summer and winter. Quito also has one of the best preserved historical city centres in the world. Prepare to step back in time as you climb towards the sky.

The **Basilica of the National Vow** is an impressive Roman Catholic church in the old town. Building started in 1892 but it isn't completed yet. Some locals say that the world will come to an end when it is finished. Look out for its unusual gargoyles which are inspired by iguanas, pumas and Galápagos tortoises.

Carondelet Palace (the Presidential Palace) is set on the square. It was built as a palace for Spanish royalty but has been used as a seat for the Government of the Republic of Ecuador since 1822. The President of Ecuador currently lives here too.

The Church and Convent of San Francisco is famous for its monks and its beautiful architecture. It's the oldest religious building in the city dating back to 1535.

HISTORY

Quito has a rich history that includes its indigenous ancient people, the Canari, the Cara and the Quitu. The Incas arrived in the fifteenth century and its leader Huayna Capac made Quito the second capital of the Inca Kingdom. The Incas were defeated by the Spanish in 1532 and San Francisco de Quito was founded in 1534, the Inca settlement having been destroyed. The colonists developed the city, building beautiful churches, monasteries and palaces. The indigenous people were treated badly, however, and in 1830 they took back control. Revolts, change of government and powerful earthquakes have shaken this city ever since.

MONEY

Ecuador's official currency is the US dollar! Ecuador changed its currency to the US dollar in 2000. Ecuador does mint its own coins (centavos) but they are the same value as US cent coins.

Fedora

THINGS TO DO

Fiesta

Wear a hat

Hats are everywhere in this city! A **fedora** hat is part of indigenous women's clothing.

Quito is the best place to pick up a genuine **Panama** hat. These popular straw hats were originally made in Ecuador. They got their name because they were worn by workers on the Panama canal. By 1944 the Panama hat was Ecuador's top export (it's now bananas!).

Take part in a fiesta

Fiesta de Quito is a colourful festival that celebrates the founding of the city by the Spanish. The festival starts in late November and goes on for a month. Parades, parties, bullfighting and live music fill the streets.

FOOD

Guinea pig ice cream

Guinea pig

Roast guinea pig (**cuy**) is one of Ecuador's traditional foods, mostly eaten on special occasions. You will find it on the menu in a few places and it is likely to be served with potatoes and peanut sauce with vegetables like oiled corn, lima beans and avocado.

How about guinea pig ice cream? Apparently, it tastes rather like chicken. There's beetle ice cream on offer too, which is usually flavoured with fruit.

Chocolate paradise

Fortunately, there are plenty of chocolate shops in Quito too! Ecuador is famous for its high-quality cacao beans – sometimes called the 'new black gold'. Dark chocolate is a speciality.

Chocolate

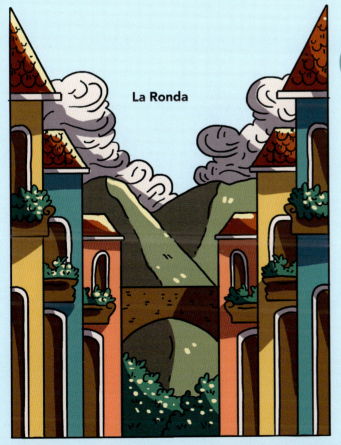

La Ronda

PLACES TO GO

Fragrant forest

Parque Metropolitano Guangüiltagua is set on the hill of Bellavista and is the largest urban park in South America. The forest is full of fragrant eucalyptus trees and you may spot the local llamas.

Art hub

La Ronda is another old part of the city which was once famous for its artists and writers. Many of the pretty Spanish-style houses were built in the eighteenth and nineteenth century. Sadly, the area fell into ruin but in 2006 La Ronda was restored. Now it's filled with life again with cafes, restaurants, art galleries and arty shops to explore.

The magnificent **Palacio Barolo** was built to represent the Divine Comedy by the Italian poet Dante (1265–1321). The basement and ground floor represent hell and the top floor is heaven. All the floors in between represent purgatory. It is 100 metres high and until 1935 was the tallest building in South America.

The **Metropolitan Cathedral** is one of the most commanding buildings in the square. The neoclassical facade with its mighty columns looks more like an ancient Roman temple than a cathedral!

The **Obelisk of Buenos Aires** was erected in 1936 and is 67,5 m high.

Cabildo de Buenos Aires on Plaza de Mayo is one of the last remaining colonial buildings in the city. It was a council building but now it is a museum.

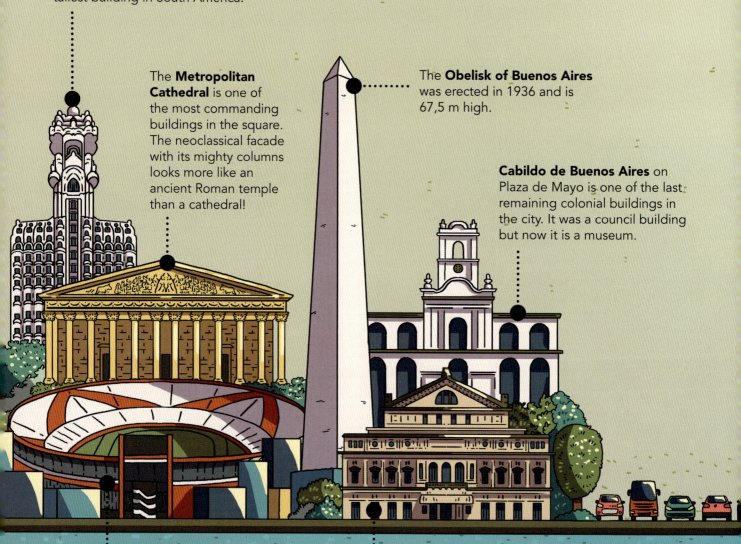

Buenos Aires sits on the south-west bank of the **River Plate.** If you say River Plate in this city, people will think you mean the football stadium. Football is a national obsession and the **River Plate Stadium** is the homeground for the Club Atlético River Plate football team.

Buenos Aires has many theatres and halls. **Teatro Colón** is one of the most famous opera houses in the world. Famous opera singers such as Enrico Caruso, Luciano Pavarotti and Maria Callas have performed in this stunning building.

BUENOS AIRES
ARGENTINA

Buenos dias from Buenos Aires, the capital of Argentina. This is a multicultural city with Spanish the most widely used language. Around 3 million people live in the city proper and 15 million in the metropolitan area. It has wide avenues, colonial buildings, football and lots of tango dancing. It is sometimes called 'the Paris of South America' and it attracts more visitors than any other city on the continent.

Palacio de Aguas Corrientes looks fit for a king. In the late nineteenth century this beautiful building had all the pipes, tanks and pumps necessary to supply the city with water so it is often called the Water Palace instead.

In recent years Buenos Aires has started to grow upwards. More skyscrapers are planned but as of 2020 the **Alvear Tower** is the tallest at 235 m – this puts it in the top five of the tallest buildings in South America.

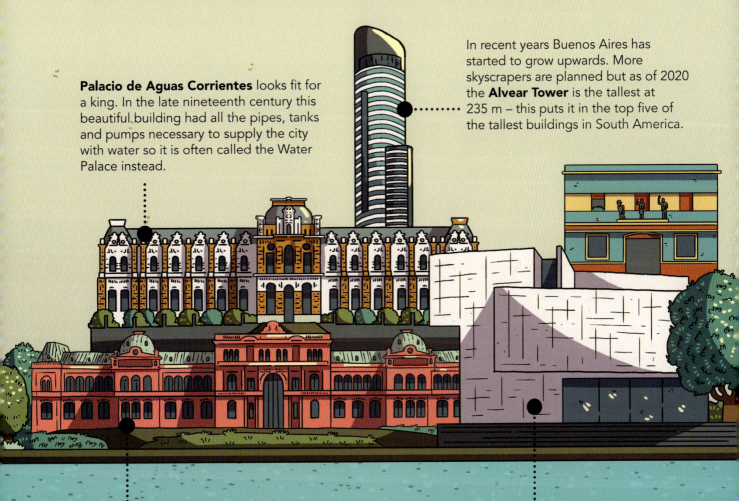

The big pink building on Plaza de Mayo is called **Casa Rosada**. Once this was a grand post office but now it is one of the official seats of the President of Argentina.

The **Latin American Art Museum of Buenos Aires (MALBA)** shows the works of modern artists from all over Latin America.

HISTORY

The Spanish settled the area that would become Buenos Aires twice. In 1536, Pedro de Mendoza first laid claim to the region but abandoned the settlement when the indigenous people attacked it to defend their land. Another settlement was established in 1580 by Juan de Garay. Situated on the shores of the estuary of the Río de la Plata, this was an ideal place for trade – so good that Britain attempted to invade the city too! The fight for power has always been part of the history of Buenos Aires. Argentina declared independence from Spain on 9 July, 1816. This day is celebrated with festivities and fireworks each year on Independence or Revolution Day. Argentines know how to party which is why so many tourists keep coming back!

MONEY

The Argentine peso (AR$) is the local currency. The head of Eva Perón (1919–1952) graces the front of the $100 note. She was the second wife of the Argentine president Juan Perón who came to power in 1946. She was the subject of the musical *Evita* and is still beloved in her country today for her activism in many areas, including women's suffrage.

PLACES TO GO

Recoleta Cemetery

A day out to a graveyard might not sound fun but it's quite normal in Argentina, where people will often picnic around the graves of their loved ones. **Recoleta Cemetery** is one of the most beautiful graveyards in the world and well worth a visit. The graves are above ground and there are hundreds of ornate mausoleums, memorials and statues to admire. One of the most famous graves belongs to Eva Perón.

Recoleta Cemetery

FOOD

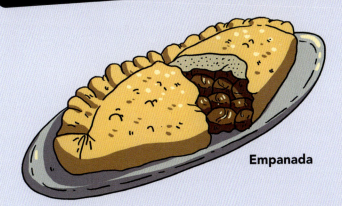

BUENOS AIRES
ARGENTINA

Empanada everywhere!

Empanada is probably the most popular food in Argentina. This pastry is shaped like a half-moon, with a braided edge. You can choose all kinds of delicious fillings, with beef, chicken, chorizo (spicy sausage), cheese or vegetables being favourites.

Empanada

Hot dog Argentinian style

Choripán is a local version of a hot dog and you'll see street vendors selling them everywhere. Chorizo is grilled on an open fire and slapped between warmed slices of bread. Chimichurri sauce on top gives it extra spice!

Choripán

THINGS TO DO

Café Tortoni

Tango at Café Tortoni

Buenos Aires is the tango capital of the world. People love to stay up late dancing and there are hundreds of dance halls (*milongas*) to visit.

The famous **Café Tortoni** is one of the best places to watch the dancers in action. Performers have been strutting, twisting, turning and doing those tango kicks here since 1880. The **National Tango Academy** is just next door and they welcome visitors too!

Sacsayhuamán (pronounced 'sak-sey-wuhman') is an Incan fortress and temple which was constructed from fifteenth century. Parts of it date back even earlier to the Killke people who lived here around 900 to 1200 CE. The walls of the fortress are created from great blocks of stone, some weighing around 113.4 tonnes. Set high on a hill, this is a wonderful place to see over the city.

Ten minutes away from Sacsayhuamán stands **Cristo Blanco**, a large statue of Jesus Christ with his arms outstretched towards the city. This statue is 8 m tall and looks spectacular when it is lit up at night.

A golden statue of **Pachacuti**, an emperor of the Inca Empire, stands on top of a fountain in Plaza de Armas. The statue was only erected in 2011 but is a reminder of the city's Incan history.

In the middle of the city stands **Plaza de Armas**. This beautiful square was a meeting place for the Incas long before the Spanish arrived in 1533. A giant rock covered in gold called 'the stone of war' was placed in the square and the Incas performed ceremonies here before going to war. Today the square has magnificent colonial buildings and is a lively hub for tourists and locals.

CUZCO
PERU

The **Church of the Society of Jesus** sits on the south-east side of Plaza de Almas on the remains of an Inca palace. Jesuits began building work here in 1576 and it took over 100 years to complete as much of the building was destroyed in the earthquake of 1650. It has a beautiful ornate façade as well as gilded wooden altars and carved balconies.

Welcome to Cuzco (Cusco) in the Peruvian Andes, one of the oldest continuously inhabited cities in South America. This beautiful city is famed for its Incan and Spanish history. Say *Allianchu* (Quechua for 'hello, how are you?') to one of the Andean locals and you'll get a big smile in return. Situated high in the Peruvian Andes at around 3,400 m, don't be surprised to find clouds hovering near your head. Many tourists come here en route to the Inca citadel of Machu Picchu, and fall in love with this intriguing ancient city.

The early Spanish settlers were impressed with the streets, buildings and stone walls made by the Incas. However, they destroyed the Inca buildings during their invasion and built their own churches and palaces in their place, using Incas to do the heavy work. **Cuzco Cathedral** stands on the northeast section of Plaza de Almas where an Inca temple once stood and many of the stones used to build it were taken from Sacsayhuamán.

HISTORY

Cuzco has been inhabited for over 3,000 years but it is the Incas and Spanish that have left their mark on this colourful city in the mountains. The Incas made the city their capital in the thirteenth century, calling it the 'navel of the world' and building it in the shape of the sacred puma. The Spanish defeated the Incas in 1533 and rebuilt the city in a colonial style. Peru took back independence from Spain in 1821 and the cultures have entwined ever since. In 1983 the city of Cuzco was declared a World Heritage Site by UNESCO. Now Cuzco is a major tourist destination, welcoming around 2 million visitors every year.

MONEY

The Peruvian nuevo sol is the official currency of Peru but most people just call it the 'sol'. Be careful – there is rumoured to be plenty of fake money here.

THINGS TO DO

Study the Twelve-Angled Stone

A walk to look at a wall might not sound that exciting, but the Incan wall on **Hatun Rumiyoc** might change your mind. All the stones are intricately cut but it's the famous Twelve-Angled Stone that fascinates people. This stone has 12 corners and 12 sides. It fits the wall perfectly and stays put without the need for concrete.

Traditional dress

Discover traditional ways to dress

Everywhere you go in Cuzco you will see people wearing brightly-coloured traditional dress. Women wear shawls (*llicllas*) with little jackets (*jobona*) and embroidered skirts (*polleras*) finished off with a hat. Men don't dress up as much, but may wear ponchos with knee-length trousers and a beanie hat.

Incan wall

FOOD

Alpaca

Anyone for roasted guinea pig?

Roasted guinea pig is often on the menu in Cuzco. The whole animal is cooked, including the ears, teeth and feet. It tastes a little like duck and it's not bad manners to eat it with your hands – that's if you want to eat it at all!

Alpaca on the menu

Alpaca steak is another delicacy enjoyed by the locals. Alpacas are similar to llamas but smaller. Mostly, they are raised for their soft wool but the meat is tender and low in fat so they are good to eat too!

Roasted guinea pig

PLACES TO GO

Cuzco Planetarium

Cuzco Planetarium

Located in the mountains, **Cuzco Planetarium** is 15 minutes away from the heart of the city. This is the perfect place to look up at the clear night sky and view the stars of the Milky Way. You will also discover how the Incas used the stars to make predictions or even design their cities.

San Pedro Market

You can buy anything from cuddly alpaca jumpers and hats to fresh fruit juices and bundles of plantains at **San Pedro Market**. Many tourists walk away with cute Pachamama dolls which are handmade by the locals.

Pachamama dolls

Montevideo is situated on the southern coast of Uruguay and on the northeastern bank of the River Plate (Buenos Aires is on its western bank). The city grew around Montevideo Bay where the busy Port of Montevideo is situated.

Montevideo has some impressive modern buildings but it's the **Telecommunications Tower** which dominates the skyline. It is 157 m high with a curved, beak-shape piercing the sky on top.

There are plenty of **river beaches** in this city and you'll find many of the locals hanging out on the gorgeous white sands. Pocitos, Carrasco, Buceo and Malvín beach are just a few hotspots filled with people sunbathing, working out, playing volleyball and football (fútbol) or enjoying the delicious fresh fish trawled from the river.

The **World Trade Center Montevideo** was completed in 2009 and is a buzzing business and culture hub in the city.

The **Rambla** is the avenue that stretches for 22 km along the coast of Montevideo. It's one of the longest beach esplanades in the world and it's perfect for strolling, cycling and rollerblading or just relaxing and watching the world go by.

Clues to Montevideo's history lie in its **Old City** (Ciudad Vieja). The city was founded between 1724 and 1726 by the Spanish, so many of the buildings look European. Tree-lined avenues and squares add to this feeling. The old town was once surrounded by a fortress but there are only a few parts remaining.

Teatro Solís was opened in 1856 and is Uruguay's oldest theatre. It was designed by an Italian architect and, with its neo-classical facade and those grand columns, it could easily pass for an Italian opera house!

MONTEVIDEO
URUGUAY

Welcome and *buenos dias* from Montevideo, the capital of Uruguay. This friendly, historical city is located across the water from Buenos Aires, the capital of Argentina. The cities share a Spanish past with people that love to tango and play football. However, Montevideo is much smaller with a population in the city proper of around 1.3 million. Life is good, the standard of living is high and Montevideo has become one of South America's most expensive cities to live in. The pace of life is much slower too; people here often raise a toast before a meal and say: *salud, dinero, amor, y tiempo para disfrutarlo* which translates as 'health, wealth, love, and the time to enjoy it'.

It may look like a crazy Art-Deco rocket or lighthouse but the **Palacio Salvo** is one of the most iconic buildings in the city. It was opened in 1928 and, standing at 100 m high, it was the tallest building in South America for a few years.

Montevideo's main square, called **Plaza Independencia** (Independence Square) is a great place to take your time and just watch the world go by. In the centre stands the **Artigas Mausoleum** where the remains of José Gervasio Artigas (known as 'the father of Uruguayan nationhood') are laid to rest.

HISTORY

One of the most obvious questions about this city is where does it get its name? One explanation is it comes from the Portuguese 'Monte vide eu' meaning 'I see a mountain'. In the eighteenth century, the Spanish and Portuguese competed for land on both sides of the River Plate but it was the Spanish soldier Bruno Mauricio de Zabala who ousted the Portuguese and claimed this spot in 1726. The city grew up around its port but always competed with Buenos Aires for trade. In the early years of the nineteenth century the city was occupied by the British, Argentine, Portuguese, Brazilian and, of course, the Spanish. Uruguay won independence in 1828 and made Montevideo the capital. The city has seen civil wars, sieges and political unrest. It has thrived and declined too but in recent years it is on the up again and is renowned for its friendly laid-back atmosphere. As they say in Montevideo, *arriba bo* (Hey you, let's go!).

MONEY

The Uruguayan peso is the unit of currency. Like many South American countries the value of currency fluctuates – which means it goes up and down. This is why some people prefer to be paid in US dollars, which is a relatively strong currency.

Tango dancers

Candombe

THINGS TO DO

Dance!

You will catch some impressive tango dancing in Montevideo – locals here claim the dance was invented on both sides of the river, not just in Buenos Aires in Argentina. Seek out tango clubs (*milongas*) for live performances or head to the streets to try yourself.

Candombe definitely belongs to Uruguay. This enchanting and energetic style of drumming and dance was brought to the country by African slaves. Now it's performed at regular gatherings in the city and especially during Carnaval in January and February.

FOOD

Hot, hot dog!

The pancho, also called the Uruguayan hot dog, has a great big sausage in the middle and it comes with some epic toppings. These include 'salsa golf' which is a mix of mayonnaise and ketchup, corn, melted cheese and spicy sauce. People often go for a side of sweet potato fries too!

Rogel cake

Pancho

Sweet dreams

The bakeries in Montevideo have a mouthwatering selection of cakes and pastries. Everything is very sweet. One of the nation's favourites is the Rogel cake or torta alfajor. Crispy layers of pastry are glued together with dulce de leche (a caramel made from milk) and smothered in meringue icing.

Escaramuza Libros

PLACES TO GO

Mercado del Puerto

The Port Market (Mercado del Puerto) is a beautiful old historical building where you can buy antiques while listening to local street musicians. This is also a great place to sample one of the city's favourite foods: barbecued steak.

Escaramuza Libros

No ordinary bookshop, this lovely old house from around 1903 is filled with books, many of which you'd need a ladder to reach. There is a cafe too, so you can sit and take in your beautiful surroundings.

Built in 1892 and 43.5 m tall, **St George Cathedral** was once the world's tallest wooden building. It may not hold that record now but it is still Georgetown's most impressive building. Inside you'll find a large chandelier that was donated by Queen Victoria (1819–1901).

St Andrew's Kirk is one of the oldest buildings in Guyana. The Dutch started building it in 1811, but ran out of money so sold it to Scottish colonists who completed it in 1818. The Scots and the Dutch shared it as a place of worship.

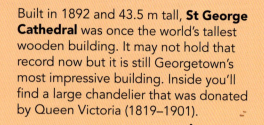

Georgetown is protected by a seawall. At high tide the city is 1 m below sea level so the wall is needed to prevent flooding. The 450-km-long wall extends for much of Guyana's coastline. Building started in 1855 after a flood washed away the governor's house. A colourful bandstand was added in 1903.

Stabroek Market is the busiest place in Guyana. As well as being a centre for shopping and trade it is also a transport hub connecting overground transport to the traffic flow on the Demerara River.

GEORGETOWN
GUYANA

Welcome to Georgetown, the capital city of Guyana, the only country in South America to have English as its official language. Guyanese Creole, a mixture of English, East Indian and African languages is often spoken, so don't be surprised to be greeted with *wha' gwan?* (what's going on?). It is a cosmopolitan city on the North Atlantic coast of South America and, with a population of 200,500, it is by far the most populated area of the country. Due to its location and its language it tends to have more of a Caribbean culture than a South American one and this is reflected in the national sport and obsession – cricket!

The **Umana Yana** is a thatched hut made from palm leaves. The 17-m-tall building is used for exhibitions and conferences. Umana Yana means 'meeting place of the people' and the design is based on the traditional benab houses of the indigenous people.

Guyana's **Parliament Building** is easy to spot because it's by far the grandest building in Georgetown and is one of two buildings in the city with a dome. It was finished in 1834 and is beautifully maintained.

HISTORY

Georgetown, named after King George III (1738–1820), was originally called Stabroek by Dutch colonisers who arrived in 1616. The area and its indigenous tribes, the Caribs and the Arawaks, were first spotted by Columbus in 1498, and later by Sir Walter Raleigh in 1596. The Dutch soon imposed slavery on the region; conditions were brutal and resulted in significant slave rebellions. In 1831 when the Dutch lost control the country was renamed by its new owners – British Guiana. Another slave rebellion and its brutal suppression in 1823 further highlighted the the horrors of slavery and it was abolished in the British Empire in 1833. Guyana finally gained its independence in 1966 and became a republic in 1970.

Cuffy statue

1763

MONEY

The Guyanese dollar is the money that you'll be spending in Georgetown. If you get a $1000-dollar bill don't get too excited as it's about enough to buy yourself a burger. If you look closely you might be able to see a watermark of a red macaw on it.

THINGS TO DO

Celebrate Cuffy

The most important slave rebellion was the 1763 Berbice uprising led by Cuffy, a man stolen from West Africa. He organised a group of 3,000 slaves and captured plantations and weapons from the Dutch. The anniversary of the rebellion is commemorated as Republic Day, which takes place on 23 February each year. Celebrations centre around the statue of Cuffy in the Square of the Revolution.

FOOD

Pepperpot

Pig trotters pepperpot

The national dish is simply called 'pepperpot'. It is usually eaten on special days and at Christmas as it takes quite a while to cook. It is a meat (anything from chicken, pork and pig trotters) stew made with a thick, black, syrupy sauce called cassareep.

Iguana curry

If you're feeling more adventurous, you may care to sample some iguana curry. Iguana supposedly tastes similar to roast duck.

Iguana curry

PLACES TO GO

Kaieteur Falls

One of the world's most spectacular waterfalls, Kaieteur Falls is the largest in terms of volume. More than an Olympic-sized swimming pool's worth of water travels over it every four seconds. You can get there with a 90-minute flight from Georgetown or a five-day trek through the jungle.

Kaieteur Falls

La Paz is situated about 3,650 metres above sea level in a canyon surrounded by the **Altiplano mountains**. On the horizon stands Illimani, the magnificent snow-covered mountain which, at 6,438 m, is the second-highest mountain in Bolivia.

Avoid the city's noisy traffic by taking La Paz's spectacular cable car system. Who needs buses when you can jump aboard **Mi Teleférico** (My Cable Car). This is the world's largest high-altitude cable car which has around 27 km of wires weaving through the skyline, setting passengers down at all parts of the city.

San Francisco Cathedral dominates the square and is decorated with a mixture of Catholic and Aymara (the indigenous people of the region) carvings. You will see a statue of Francis of Assisi alongside carvings of snakes, dragons, tropical birds and the Inca goddess Pachamama. The church was completed in 1784 and was made into a basilica in 1948.

Plaza San Francisco is the main square in the old town of La Paz. It is the largest open public space in the city and has been the scene of political gatherings and even the Revolution which shook Bolivia for three days in 1952.

LA PAZ
BOLIVIA

La Paz Cathedral is built on a steep hill and features a dome and two towers. It took around 100 years to construct this beautiful neoclassical-style cathedral.

'Honk! honk!' watch out, you're going to get caught in lots of traffic jams in the chaotic capital of La Paz in Bolivia. It has a small population of around 790,000 but most of them seem to be on the road! This is the highest capital city in the world so you'll need a head for heights too. With its incredible scenery, beautiful colonial buildings, amazing markets and vibrant street life, it is well worth a visit.

La Paz has some impressive modern buildings. Many are influenced by indigenous architecture and art, so they have a completely unique look.

Plaza Murillo is the central square in the city where many of its finest colonial buildings are located. You'll find the **Presidential Palace**, National Congress of Bolivia and La Paz Cathedral on this beautiful, bustling square.

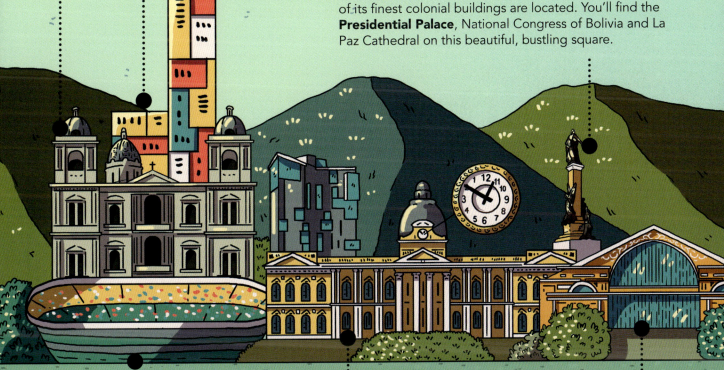

Estadio Hernando Siles is the largest stadium in Bolivia and one of highest, in terms of altitude, sport complexes in the world. Many of the city's major football teams play matches here, including The Strongest, Bolivia's oldest football team.

The **National Congress of Bolivia** is famous for the clock which has its numbers reversed – the one to 12 go in an anti-clockwise direction.

La Paz bus station was designed by Gustave Eiffel who also created the Eiffel Tower in Paris.

HISTORY

It is gold that brought people to live on these steep hills in the Andes. Originally, it was just local Aymara miners up here. Then in 1548 the Spanish invaded and founded the city they called La Ciudad de Nuestra Señora de La Paz or 'the City of Our Lady of Peace'. The indigenous people were expected to adopt the Spanish way of life, including their religion. Inevitably, there was conflict and uprisings and the city wasn't as peaceful as its name suggested. Bolivia gained independence from Spain in 1825 and La Paz prospered, becoming the administrative capital in 1898. Revolution and unrest have always gripped this city but it is one of the most popular tourist destinations in South America ...

MONEY

The boliviano is the official currency of Bolivia. Since 2018, a new family of banknotes has gradually been introduced. This colourful collection portrays national heroes as well as beautiful natural landscapes and animals of Bolivia.

PLACES TO GO

Witches' Market

If you're looking for love, luck or good health then you should head to **La Paz Witches' Market**. The market is run by witch doctors called *yatiri* and they sell all kinds of potions and ingredients to make spells. Dried frogs and turtles, powdered dog's tongue and various medicinal herbs are on offer. Llama foetuses are popular too and are buried in the foundations of new buildings to keep people safe.

Witches' Market

FOOD

Street food

La Paz has lots of tempting street food including pastries and choripán (chorizo and bread) but it also has some fairly unusual food to go.

- **Anticucho** is cow's heart kebab and it comes with spicy peanut sauce and potatoes.
- **Tripa** is fried cow's intestine which is rather chewy and eaten with lots of spicy peanut sauce.
- **Ají de Lengua** is cow's tongue. It's slimy as well as chewy!
- **Ispi** are tiny fish from Lake Titicaca. They are deep fried and served whole.

Ispi

THINGS TO DO

Watch zebras crossing

Young people wearing zebra costumes out on the streets of La Paz are there to help you cross the busy roads. The **Zebra Urban Educators programme** was introduced in 2001 to show people the crosswalks and where it's safe to cross the road. The idea has been so successful that it's caught on in other cities in Bolivia.

All around the city you will see indigenous Aymara and Quechua women called '**cholitas**'. Usually, they wear a wide puffed skirt called 'la pollera' and bowler hats. Until recently, these women were not allowed to travel on public transport or go into some public places. Since 2006, and the election of Evo Morales, the first indigenous president of Bolivia, they have more freedom.

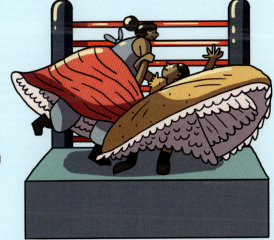

Cholita wrestling

See cholitas

Cholita wrestling is now a popular form of entertainment in the city. The wrestling is choreographed which means that it isn't real fighting. Often the women are from poor backgrounds and this is a way for them to make money to support their families.

MORE SOUTH AMERICAN CITIES

PARAMARIBO, SURINAME

Paramaribo is the capital city of Suriname, South America's smallest country. Dutch colonists established a trading post here in 1613. Later, English settlers proclaimed it the capital in 1650. The Dutch took back control in 1667. The country gained independence in 1975 but Dutch remains the most widespread language. Its beautiful Dutch colonial buildings are well preserved and the city has been declared a UNESCO World Heritage Site.

Population: 240,924 (2021)
Highest building: Wyndham Garden Hotel (32 m)
Places to see: Presidential Palace of Suriname, St Peter and St Paul Cathedral, Arya Dewaker Hindu Temple, Fort Zeelandia

SANTA CRUZ, BOLIVIA

The modern world meets the past on the streets of Santa Cruz, Bolivia's largest city and one of the fastest-growing urban areas in the world. The city was established by Spanish colonists on the Pirai River in 1561. Beautiful Spanish buildings survive to this day but since the 1990s the skyline has been changing with more office blocks and apartments shooting up.

Population: 1.75 million (2021)
Highest building: Condominio La Casona (127 m)
Places to see: Basilica Menor de San Lorenzo, Manzana Uno (art centre), Biocentro Guembe Mariposario

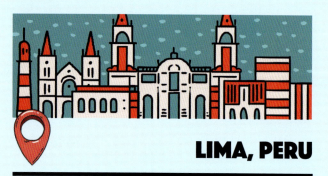

LIMA, PERU

The capital of Peru was established by the Spanish in 1535. The Spanish originally named it Ciudad de los Reyes (the City of Kings) but the name Lima probably came from the local Ichma language. Situated on cliffs over the coastline, this is the third-largest city in South America. This lively city has it all including beaches, beautiful colonial buildings, Inca ruins and traffic!

Population: 9.75 million (2021)
Highest building: Torre Rimac (208 m)
Places to see: Plaza de Armas de Lima, Huaca Pucllana, Basilica y Convento de San Francisco

MANAUS, BRAZIL

In the middle of the Amazon rainforest stands the city of Manaus. In the nineteenth century people came here to tap the rubber which at the time was like striking gold! Beautiful buildings like the Amazon Theatre were erected. After the rubber boom the city fell into poverty – the electricity went off and the beloved theatre closed for 90 years. Since the 1960s, the city has started to recover and was one of the host cities for 2014 FIFA World Cup.

Population: 2.30 million (2021)
Highest building: Manaus Shopping Centre (110 m)
Places to see: Amazonas Opera House, Meeting of Waters (the confluence of the Negro River and the Amazon River), Ponta Negra beach

CUENCA, ECUADOR

Sometimes Cuenca is called the 'Athens of Ecuador' because it is a centre of culture and art. It has also been declared a UNESCO World Heritage Site because of its charming historical centre which was founded in 1557 by the Spanish. It's located in the southern Andes on a confluence of four rivers, so there are plenty of natural wonders to explore too.

Population: 427,315 (2021)

Highest building: Edificio Camara de Industrias de Cuenca (53 m)
Places to see: New Cathedral of Cuenca, El Cajas National Park, Museo Pumapungo.

CARTAGENA, COLOMBIA

The city of Cartagena has the Caribbean Sea and an impressive Old Town that is a UNESCO World Heritage Site. The area had been settled by indigenous peoples since ancient times, but after the arrival of Spanish colonists in 1533, Cartagena became the major port between Spain and its empire, trading mostly in silver and slaves from Africa. In those days Cartagena attracted pillaging pirates but now it's tourists who visit this beautifully-preserved walled city.

Population: 1,070,692 (2021)
Highest building: Hotel Estelar (202 m)
Places to see: Castillo de San Felipe de Barajas, El Totumo (bubbling mud volcano), Convento De La Popa, Palace of the Inquisition

POTOSÍ, BOLIVIA

Potosí was founded in 1545 by the Spanish when silver ore was discovered in the Cerro Rico ('Rich Mountain'). During the silver boom Potosí became the richest and largest city in South America although many of the miners died working in appalling conditions. Many beautiful colonial churches and buildings were commissioned and the city was home to the Spanish colonial mint. Many of these buildings survive today.

Population: 219,040 (2021)
Places to see: Potosí Cathedral, Potosí Mint (Casa de la Moneda), La Capilla de Nuestra Señora de Jerusalén

ASUNCIÓN, PARAGUAY

Asunción is one of the longest inhabited cities on the Rio de la Plata Basin so it has earned the name the 'Mother of Cities'. It was founded in 1537 by the Spanish and was a centre of colonial rule when Buenos Aires was reclaimed by indigenous peoples in 1542. The city has had its own share of revolts and fights for independence. Today, the capital of Paraguay has some fabulous yet slightly crumbling colonial buildings to explore. Tourists enjoy its riverside location and exciting cultural scene.

Population: 3.39 million (2021)
Highest building: The Icono Tower (136 m)
Places to see: Mercado Cuatro, Palacio de los López, Casa de la Independencia, Museo del Barro, Panteón Nacional de los Héroes

GLOSSARY

capybara
a large South American rodent that looks rather like a long-legged guinea pig.

civil war
a war between people living in the same country.

colonist/colonial
a member of a group of people who have taken political control of a region/style of food or architecture created by colonists.

cosmopolitan
describes a place where there are people from many different countries.

foetus
the unborn baby of an animal.

funicular
a railway that goes up and down a slope or mountain by cable.

indigenous
a person or thing that is naturally occurring or originated in a particular place.

Lent
the forty days before Easter when some Christians fast or give up something they enjoy to remember when Christ fasted in the wilderness.

mausoleum
a building that houses the tombs of the rich or famous.

metropolitan
describes the area over which a large city has power and influence, including its suburbs and even neighbouring towns.

neoclassical
describes art, architecture, literature or music that copies the style of the ancient Greeks and Romans.

pilgrimage
the journey to a sacred place by a religious person (pilgrim).

plateau
an area of very high ground where the top is flat and level.

security services
a governmental organisation set up to protect a country against secret plots and terrorist threats.

temperate
describes the climate in a region that is never too hot or too cold and has moderate rainfall spread throughout the year.

UNESCO World Heritage Site
a place or building that is protected and preserved by the United Nations Educational, Scientific and Cultural Organization (UNESCO).

INDEX